TALES FROM

№ 3

MAPLE RIDGE

THE BIG CITY

By Grace Gilmore
Illustrated by Petra Brown

LITTLE SIMON
NEW YORK   LONDON   TORONTO   SYDNEY   NEW DELHI

LITTLE SIMON
An imprint of Simon & Schuster Children's Publishing Division
1230 Avenue of the Americas, New York, New York 10020
This Little Simon edition June 2015
Copyright © 2015 by Simon & Schuster, Inc.
All rights reserved, including the right of reproduction in whole or in part in any form.
LITTLE SIMON is a registered trademark of Simon & Schuster, Inc., and associated colophon is a trademark of Simon & Schuster, Inc.
For information about special discounts for bulk purchases, please contact Simon & Schuster Special Sales at 1-866-506-1949 or business@simonandschuster.com.
The Simon & Schuster Speakers Bureau can bring authors to your live event. For more information or to book an event, contact the Simon & Schuster Speakers Bureau at 1-866-248-3049 or visit our website at www.simonspeakers.com.
Designed by Chani Yammer
The illustration of this book were rendered in pen and ink.
The text of this book was set in Caecilia.
Manufactured in the United States of America 0515 FFG
10 9 8 7 6 5 4 3 2 1
Library of Congress Cataloging-in-Publication Data
Gilmore, Grace.
The big city / by Grace Gilmore ; illustrated by Petra Brown. — First edition. pages cm. — (Tales from Maple Ridge ; [3])
Summary: Logan Pryce and his father spend a day in the big city of Sherman, but despite his eagerness to leave "boring" Maple Ridge, Logan is glad to return to quiet, familiar surroundings after the hustle and bustle of the city.
[1. City and town life—Fiction. 2. Contentment—Fiction. 3. Family life—Fiction. 4. Farm life—Fiction.] I. Brown, Petra, illustrator. II. Title. PZ7.G4372Big 2015 [Fic]—dc23 2014017735
ISBN 978-1-4814-3007-4 (hc) ISBN 978-1-4814-3006-7 (pbk) ISBN 978-1-4814-3008-1 (eBook)

CONTENTS

CHAPTER 1

◦ LOGAN'S BIG TRIP ◦

Logan Pryce dipped his net into the pond and swished it through the water.

"Got you!" he shouted.

He reached into the net and grabbed a fat green frog. It wiggled out of his fist and hopped back into the pond with a loud *splash!*

Next to Logan, his best friend,

Anthony Bruna, laughed. "Gosh, that's the sixth frog that's gotten away from you today."

Logan grinned. "Oh, well! I'm bored of catching frogs anyway."

"Bored? But you *love* catching frogs."

"Maybe when I was seven. That was a long time ago."

"A *long time ago?*" Anthony rolled his eyes.

The two boys picked up their nets and rose to their feet. The pond was at the far end of the Pryce family's farm—or rather, their  *former* farm. A few months ago, Mr. Pryce had decided to give up farming so he could find a job with better pay.

In fact, he was going to Sherman tomorrow to see about a position

at Garrison's Glass Works. He was taking Logan with him so they could visit with Logan's uncle and aunt and cousins.

Logan couldn't wait! He hadn't been to Sherman in many years, so he didn't remember much about it. Still, he was sure it would be much more exciting than Maple Ridge. Their town was so small that it wasn't even on the map of the United States at their school.

"What do you want to do now?" asked Anthony. "Go fishing in the creek? Walk over to the general store? I think I have a penny to buy candy." He dug through his dungaree pockets.

"I should probably go pack for my big trip," said Logan.

"Big trip? How long will you be in Sherman?"

"Pa and I leave bright and early tomorrow morning, and we'll be back by suppertime."

"Well, you'd better pack a couple of suitcases, then," Anthony teased him.

"Ha-ha!"

They started walking across the lush green meadow. The ground was soft beneath their bare feet. Cabbage whites and monarchs flitted among the daisies and cornflowers. In the distance, Lightning and Buttercup, the Pryces' horses, grazed in the warm sun.

Soon, the Pryce house came

into view. Logan spotted Pa in the backyard, playing hoops with the girls. Tess was nine, a year older than Logan. Annie was four.

Anthony followed Logan's gaze

with a wistful look. "My papa's at the factory today. He probably won't be home till late."

"Aw, that's too bad." Logan knew that Anthony's father worked long hours at a steel mill in Sherman.

For a moment, Logan felt uneasy about the idea of Pa working in Sherman too. Would he still have time to spend with their family?

Logan tried to push his doubts aside as he hooked his arm through Anthony's. "I almost forgot. Today is baking day. Ma made shortbread cookies!" he said cheerfully.

Anthony's face lit up. "Gosh, really? Shortbread cookies are my favorite."

"To the kitchen, then!"

"To the kitchen!"

Laughing, they hurried their steps.

• GETTING READY •

"Do you have the presents Annie and I made for our cousins?" Tess asked Logan during breakfast the next morning.

Logan peered into his gunnysack. "Check!"

"Your coin purse?"

He reached into the sack and pulled out an old sock containing

two nickels. "Check!"

"Your comb?"

Logan frowned. "My *comb*?"

"You'd be wise to bring your comb, Logan. City folks are very neat and fashionable," Tess informed him.

"Fash-ion-able? What does that mean?" asked Logan.

"It means you can't go to the big city with your hair looking like a sparrow's nest," their older brother, Drew, joked as he strolled into the kitchen. He was eleven and thought he knew everything.

Annie skipped in behind Drew. "Sparrow? Where's a sparrow?" she cried out in delight.

"My hair does *not* look like a sparrow's nest!" Logan reached up and smoothed down his unruly blond locks.

"Children, please!" Ma turned from the cast-iron stove, where she was stirring a pot of porridge.

"Pa and Logan need to be on their way soon. Drew, please go get Pa and let him know his breakfast's ready. I think he's outside hitching up Lightning to the buggy."

"Did I hear someone mention breakfast?"

Pa stood in the back door. His hair was slicker and shinier than usual, and his cheeks were freshly shaved and ruddy. He was dressed in his Sunday suit, even though it wasn't a Sunday.

"You look very fash-ion-able, Pa," Logan told him.

"Why, thank you, son!" Pa said, beaming.

As Pa sat down at the table, he carefully tucked a napkin under his shirt collar. Annie climbed up into his lap. "Mrs. Wigglesworth wants a story," she said, holding up her cloth doll.

Pa dug into his porridge and began reciting the tale of the three little pigs. The other children

listened too, even though they were too old for such tales. The kerosene lamp cast a golden glow on all their faces. The family dog, Skeeter, napped by the stove and thumped his tail contentedly.

And then it was time to leave. Pa and Logan hugged everyone and said their good-byes.

Ma pressed a bundle into Pa's hands. "I baked some biscuits. You two have a long ride ahead of you."

"They smell wonderful, Alice," said Pa.

Skeeter trotted up to Logan and
regarded him with sad eyes. Logan
bent down to pet him. "Aw, Skeeter.
I'll bring back a city treat for you,"
he promised.

"It's time, Logan!" Pa called out.

Logan pulled on his boots and grabbed his gunnysack. He followed Pa outside to where Lightning and the buggy awaited them.

Sherman, here we come! Logan thought eagerly.

CHAPTER 3

ARRIVING
IN SHERMAN

Two hours later, Pa and Logan pulled into downtown Sherman.

"What do you think, son?" Pa asked as he steered their buggy onto a wide, bustling street called Broad Boulevard.

"It's swell!" Logan exclaimed. "It's better than swell! It's ... it's ... it's ..." He was at a loss for words.

Logan couldn't stop staring. Downtown Sherman was nothing like downtown Maple Ridge. Crowds of people dressed in city finery walked briskly on cement sidewalks. Shiny new coaches with elegant horses rolled along the cobblestone pavement. Street vendors sold goods from carts, yelling things like: *"Raspberries! Strawberries! Get your fresh berries!"*

Two bays trotted by, pulling a strange-looking carriage the size of a railroad car. Lightning flinched and gave a snort. Inside the carriage, a dozen people sat on wooden benches. A bell clanged, and a man in a black cap leaned out and shouted, "Next stop, Majestic Hotel!"

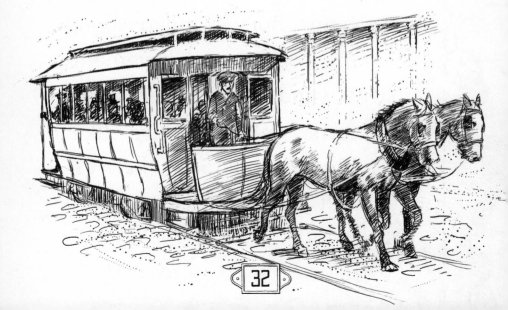

"Wh—what . . .
is . . . that?" Logan stammered.

Pa chuckled. "That's a streetcar.
It carries passengers from place
to place. The man in the cap is the
conductor."

"Wow!"

As they continued down Broad Boulevard, Logan admired the Majestic Hotel, the Carnegie Library, the opera house, and Saywell's

Department Store. Just past city hall was the Sherman Common School, which was much bigger than the one-room schoolhouse in Maple Ridge.

Beyond Broad Boulevard and to the west was a row of factories. Dark smoke puffed out of tall chimney stacks and hung thickly in the air.

"Is that where your interview is?" asked Logan, pointing.

"Yes, but I'm dropping you off at your aunt and uncle's first," replied Pa.

"Why can't I come with you?"

"This is an important job interview, and I need to speak with Mr. Garrison alone. But you'll have a good time with your cousins, and I'll come by as soon as I'm finished."

"Oh, okay," Logan said with a pout.

They left Lightning and the buggy at a livery stable, then started for Aunt Violet and Uncle Archie's house on foot. Luckily, Pa knew the way. Logan found the geography of Sherman very confusing.

Pa and Logan turned onto First Street. The crowded cement sidewalks gradually turned into wooden ones. There were no shops or offices there, just grand homes and stately elm trees.

Halfway down the block, the Pryces passed a man and a woman who were out for a stroll. The man wore a fine suit and carried a cane. The woman wore a frilly bonnet and carried a parasol.

"Good day." Pa tipped his soft felt farmer's hat.

The couple frowned—first at Pa's hat, then at Logan's outfit. Logan glanced down, wondering if he'd gotten mud on his knickers. He hadn't.

"Yes, good day," the man

said in a not-so-friendly voice. He and the woman kept walking.

"Did I do something wrong?" Logan whispered to Pa.

Pa draped his arm around Logan's shoulder. "No, son. You didn't do anything wrong. City folks can be like that sometimes."

Like what? Logan wondered.

CHAPTER 4

VISITING WITH THE COUSINS

The Kelly family lived in a big white house at the end of First Street. It had graceful columns and a wide porch with wicker chairs. Neatly trimmed rosebushes bordered the front walk. Water trickled from a cast-iron fountain.

A young woman in a maid's uniform greeted them at the door.

"You must be the Pryces. Mrs. Kelly is expecting you."

"Thank you," said Pa. He and Logan stepped into the front hall.

A crystal chandelier glittered overhead. Paintings of horses and princely lords covered the gold walls.

"Hello, hello!" Aunt Violet came rushing down the hall. She hugged Logan and kissed him on both cheeks. Her perfume smelled like flowers. She had the same chestnut-brown hair as Ma, except that hers was swept up with jeweled pins.

"Alice sends her regards," Pa told Aunt Violet as they hugged.

"Archie is at the courthouse today. But he promised to try to come home early so he could visit with you and Logan," Aunt Violet said.

She turned with a swish of her skirts. "Bridget, could you get our guests some lemonade?"

Bridget gave a curtsy and disappeared down the hall. Logan blinked in surprise. Back home, he had to get his *own* lemonade!

Footsteps pounded down the stairs.

"Uncle Dale! Cousin Logan!" Clementine, who was six, threw herself against the Pryces and hugged them fiercely. She carried a doll whose pink silk dress matched hers exactly. Freddy was right behind his sister.

At fourteen, he was almost as tall as Aunt Violet. In his velvet knickers, jacket, and bow tie, he looked like one of the princely lords in the paintings. "Gentlemen, it's very nice to see you both," he said, shaking Pa's hand and then Logan's.

"Why don't we all sit for a bit in the parlor?" Aunt Violet suggested.

Logan wasn't sure what a parlor was. It turned out to be a room with lots of fancy chairs, tables, and lamps. There was a piano at one end and a marble fireplace at the other.

Everyone sat down. Reaching into his gunnysack, Logan pulled out two small packages and handed them to his cousins. "These are from Tess and Annie."

Clementine ripped hers open. A square of linen embroidered with the letter C fluttered out. "Hooray, it's a tablecloth for dolls!" she cried out. "We can use it for our tea party, Logan!"

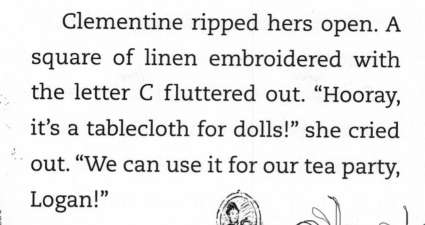

"Our . . . tea party?" Logan slowly repeated.

Freddy opened his package more slowly. His also contained a linen square, except that it had the letter *F* on it. "A handkerchief—how thoughtful!" he said. He tucked it into his jacket pocket.

Bridget appeared, carrying a silver tray with glasses of lemonade. Pa drank his quickly, then stood up to go. "I must get over to the factory for my interview."

"Of course.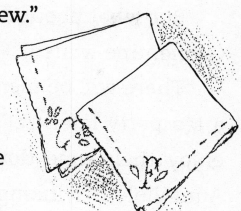
We'll take
good care
of Logan while
you're gone,"
Aunt Violet promised.

"I thought I'd show
him around Sherman,"
Freddy offered.

Logan perked up.
A tour of Sherman
with his big
cousin? What
could be better?

"But what about our tea party?" Clementine wailed.

"There will be plenty of time for a tea party later. Let's let the boys enjoy their time downtown," said Aunt Violent, winking at Logan.

"Good luck, Pa!" Logan called out, waving wildly.

Pa smiled. "Thanks, son. I'll take all the luck I can get!"

WORM CHARMERS AND MONKEYS

A while later, Logan and Freddy walked down to Broad Boulevard.

"I thought we'd stroll around a bit, then have lunch at a restaurant," said Freddy.

A *restaurant?* Logan had never been to one of those before!

The cousins proceeded down the busy street. People jostled one another on the crowded sidewalk and spilled out onto the cobblestone. A man passed by wearing a sign that said COME SEE THE WORM CHARMERS OF INDISTAN! Another man carried a monkey on his shoulder.

"Is that a pet monkey? And what are worm charmers?" Logan asked Freddy.

"That man makes his monkey perform tricks for money," replied Freddy. "Worm charmers are part of the circus, and they make their worms perform tricks too."

"Really? Wow!"

They continued walking. Logan noticed that there was a separate store for everything: a grocery store, a medicine store, a men's clothing store, and so on. In Maple Ridge, there was only one store: Mayberry's

General Store, which sold
everything from meat and
vegetables to dungarees
and farm tools.

"Freddy Kelly!"

Freddy and Logan turned. Two pretty girls pranced up to them.

"Why, hello, ladies!" Freddy looked happy suddenly.

One of the girls elbowed him. "Aren't you going to introduce us to your friend?"

"Yes, of course! Mary, Ida . . . this is my cousin Logan Pryce. He's visiting from Maple Ridge. Logan, these are my schoolmates, Mary Tilson and Ida Billingsley."

"Where's Maple Ridge? I've never heard of it," said the girl named Ida.

"It's a couple of hours from here,
in the country," explained Freddy.

"The country? How quaint!"
Mary giggled.

Logan had no idea what "quaint" meant. Was it a good thing or a bad thing?

"Say, Freddy! Did you hear about Herbert Hutchins?" asked Ida.

Freddy shook his head. "Gosh, no. Did something happen to him?"

"Did it ever!" Ida leaned closer to Freddy and whispered something in his ear. Mary joined the huddle. The

three of them burst out laughing.

Logan squirmed and shuffled his feet. Had they forgotten about him?

Sighing, he gazed into the distance.

A strange sight caught his eye.

Just down the block was a small buggy—except that it wasn't a buggy exactly. What could it be?

CHAPTER 6

THE HORSELESS CARRIAGE

Logan was very curious about the mysterious buggy-that-wasn't-a-buggy. "Hey, do you guys see that thing?" he called out.

But Freddy and his friends were still huddling and whispering.

"Okay . . . well . . . I'm going to take a look, and I'll be right back!" said Logan.

He hurried toward the vehicle. People had gathered around it and were buzzing excitedly. Inside, a man sat in a padded seat.

"What kind of buggy is this, anyway?" Logan asked a woman next to him.

"It's not a buggy. It's a horseless carriage!" she replied.

A *horseless carriage?* Logan had never heard of such a thing!

"Mr. Quincy is an inventor. He built his horseless carriage out of scraps and spare parts in his shop. Isn't it marvelous?" the woman gushed.

Logan thought about his Fix-It Shop, which was in their barn back

home. It, too, was filled with scraps and spare parts. Maybe he could build a horseless carriage someday?

Mr. Quincy began to push levers and pump his legs. Steam whooshed out of a pipe. There was a loud clanking sound, then another.

A moment later, the horseless carriage sputtered and began to crawl forward!

The crowd cheered and trotted alongside it. Logan followed, his heart racing. A machine that could move all by itself! He couldn't wait to tell Pa—and Anthony and Tess and everyone else.

Logan trailed after the horseless carriage for several more blocks. Eventually, it picked up speed and disappeared in a puff of steam.

Grinning, Logan turned to make

his way back to Freddy. He halted in his tracks, confused.

This stretch of Broad Boulevard didn't look familiar. Where was he?

He looked for the woman from before, but she was gone. "Excuse me," he said, tapping a man on the arm. "Can you tell me how to get back to . . . I think there was a barbershop . . . and something about a worm charmer. . . ."

The man scowled at him and kept walking.

Logan tugged on another person's sleeve, then another. "Excuse me? Excuse me?" he cried out. But no one stopped.

Fighting back panic, Logan tried to remember which direction he had come from. He craned his neck right and left, searching for anything that might seem familiar.

He saw the row of factories in the distance. Black smoke spewed from their chimneys and seeped

across the horizon. Even from this far away, Logan could smell soot and chemicals.

He tried to think. Those factories had been to the west when he and Pa rode into town.

He took off running.

CHAPTER 7

• LOST! •

Logan ran as fast as his legs could carry him. His gunnysack bounced sharply against his side. His lungs and muscles hurt.

He passed a jewelry shop . . . and a leather goods store . . . and a diner. He passed a poster that said THE IDEAL BRAIN TONIC! and another one that said COME TO DIXON'S DIME

MUSEUM! He didn't recognize any of it.

And then Logan saw a signpost for Fifth Street and slowed his steps. Did that mean First Street was only four blocks away, after Fourth, Third, and Second Streets?

Logan felt a flicker of hope. He remembered that the Kellys lived on First Street. Their house was white

with columns. Cousin Clementine was inside, waiting for Logan to return so they could have a tea party with her dolls. . . .

Someone bumped into him, hard. He stumbled to the ground.

"Watch where you're going!" an older boy yelled at him.

Logan's eyes filled with tears. He stood up slowly and brushed the dirt off his knickers.

I have to get out of here, he thought. *I have to find First Street. Or at least find Freddy.*

He started to run again—and stopped. He realized in alarm that he was all turned around. Had he been going *this* way before?

Or *that* way? He couldn't use the factories as a beacon anymore because a line of tall buildings blocked them from his view. Where was the sign for Fifth Street? Wasn't that the same jewelry shop he passed a few minutes ago?

86

Overwhelmed, Logan staggered over to a nearby building and sank down on the stoop. What was he going to do? Would he ever find First Street or Cousin Freddy?

Just this morning, Sherman had seemed so new and thrilling. Now it just felt like a bad dream. The downtown was crowded and noisy, full of blaring horns and street vendors shouting over one another. The air smelled like factory smoke. The people were rude and mean.

Suddenly, Logan missed his hometown with a longing that made his heart ache. He missed the peace and quiet. He missed the fresh air and green grass. He missed catching frogs with Anthony. He missed Tess and Ma and Annie and even Drew.

He covered his face with his hands and began crying.

"Logan? Is that you?" someone called out.

Logan sniffled and then peeked through his fingers to see who it was.

It was Freddy!

◉ OUT TO LUNCH ◉

"Logan! Am I ever glad I found you! I've been looking everywhere for you," said Freddy.

"You have?" Logan swiped at his eyes with the back of his sleeve. He didn't want Freddy to see that he'd been crying.

"You shouldn't wander around the city alone. You don't know your way, and besides, you're liable to run into shysters and pickpockets."

"What are those?"

"People who will lie to you and steal from you. Father says Sherman is full of them." Freddy stared at Logan. "You look pretty shaken up. Here, take my handkerchief."

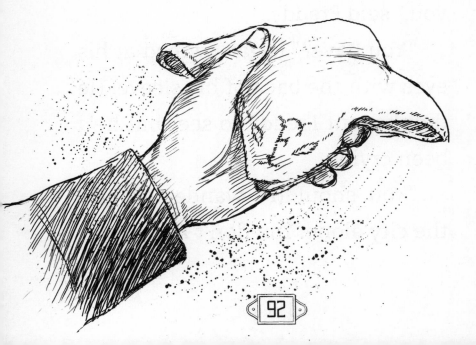

He reached into his jacket pocket and pulled out the linen square with the letter *F* on it. Logan took it and dabbed his face with it. It had a faint, familiar smell, like fresh hay and oatmeal soap. It reminded him of home and made him feel a little better.

Freddy took Logan's hand to help him up.

"Now come on, let's get you some lunch. I know a good restaurant that's just around the corner," Freddy said.

Lunch at a restaurant! Logan had almost forgotten. He smiled, definitely feeling better now.

At the restaurant, the two boys sat at the counter and ordered from a menu. It read:

JOE'S DINER

Griddle Cakes and Syrup.........................5¢

Ham and Cheese Sandwich.....................5¢

Oyster Stew...10¢

Fried Fish..10¢

Pork Chop...10¢

Meats..10¢

Slice of Cake or Pie................................5¢

Both Logan and Freddy ordered milk, ham and cheese sandwiches, and chocolate cake. As they ate the delicious food, Logan told Freddy about the horseless carriage.

"We sure don't have those in Maple Ridge," Logan finished.

"I haven't been to Maple Ridge in ages. What is it like these days?" asked Freddy.

"Well . . . it's not a big, fancy city like Sherman. But the people are nice. And our school is nice. We all helped to fix it up, so it looks practically brand new." Logan paused and thought for a moment. "Our farm is nice too. It's not really a farm anymore, but we have horses and cows and chickens and a vegetable garden. Oh, and we have this

pond where my friend Anthony
and I catch frogs. We like to
go swimming there too, and
sometimes my dog, Skeeter, swims
with us."

"I wish we had a dog. Mother and Father won't allow pets in the house," Freddy said with a sad shrug.

Logan frowned. No pets in the house? He couldn't imagine his life without Skeeter.

"Maple Ridge sounds pretty swell. Maybe I could

visit later this summer?" Freddy
suggested.

"Really?"

"Really!"

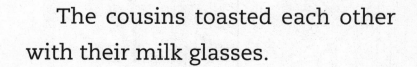

The cousins toasted each other
with their milk glasses.

CHAPTER 9

LOGAN SPENDS HIS NICKELS

As they left the restaurant, Logan noticed a boy kneeling on the ground and polishing a gentleman's shoes. He looked to be no more than six years old. His clothes were dirty and ragged, and he was barefoot. Next to him was a tin can with a few coins in it.

"What is he doing?" Logan

whispered to Freddy.

"Why, he's working, of course."

"He's a little kid!"

"In the city, many children have to work rather than go to school. Even children his age," Freddy explained.

"But I thought most people in Sherman were rich, like—" Logan hesitated. "Like our family? No. We're very lucky that Father does well as a lawyer. Clementine and I have fine clothes and music lessons and tutors to help us with

our homework. But not everyone
has what we have."

Logan considered this. His own
family was definitely far from rich.
They barely scraped by on the

money Pa earned from odd jobs here and there. That's why the interview at the glass factory was so important to him.

Still, Pa and Ma would never let their children give up school in

order to work—not even Drew, who was always hankering for a full-time job.

Logan thought for a moment. He reached into his gunnysack and got the two nickels from his coin purse.

He had been saving the money to buy souvenirs for his family and Anthony and Skeeter, but they would understand.

He dropped the nickels into the little boy's tin cup.

The boy glanced up at him in surprise. "Do you want your shoes shined, sir?"

"No, it's a present," said Logan
kindly. "And I'm not a 'sir.' I'm just
like you."

CHAPTER 10

THERE'S NO PLACE LIKE HOME

Ma had just put supper on the table when Pa and Logan walked through the door.

Skeeter jumped up to lick Logan's face. "Hey there, boy. It's nice to see you too!" Logan said, laughing.

"Lolo!" Annie leapt up from her chair and threw her arms around Logan. "It took you forever to

get home! I missed you!
Mrs. Wiggleworth's eye is
falling off!"

"I'll fix it for you
first thing," Logan
promised.

Ma hugged Pa and gazed up at
his face. "So? How did it go?"

"I think it went well," replied Pa.
"Mr. Garrison promised
to let me
know
by post
within
a week
or so."

"And how is my dear sister?"

"Violet and the family send their love."

Everyone sat down at the table and helped themselves to bacon, eggs, and fresh beans from the garden.

Tess turned to Logan eagerly. "How was Sherman? Did you meet any famous people? How did Freddy and Clementine like our presents?"

"They liked your presents!" said Logan through a mouthful of beans. He hadn't realized how hungry he was. "Clementine and I used her handkerchief to play tea party with her dolls. And Freddy says he wants to visit Maple Ridge this summer."

"Why would he want to come here? There's nothing to do," Drew pointed out.

"There's plenty to do!" Logan insisted. "Catch frogs, go swimming, play hoops in the backyard . . ."

Drew pretended to yawn. "Bor-ing!"

"That's what I used to think

too," said Logan. "Sherman *is* pretty grand. I even saw a horseless carriage there! But all in all, I think Maple Ridge is the best place in the whole entire world."

"A *horseless carriage?*" Drew, Tess, Annie, and Ma cried out at the same time.

"Yes!"

Logan told them all about the vehicle. He told them about his other adventures in Sherman too. As he talked, he realized he wanted to go back to Sherman someday. The next time, he would know better what to expect. He would try to enjoy the good things about the big city and accept the bad things.

But for now, he was just happy to be home in Maple Ridge with his family and Skeeter. And he couldn't wait to go frog catching with Anthony again!

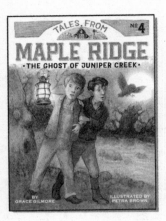

Tess frowned at the sky. "The sun's starting to go down."

"I guess we'd better head on home, then. Wait, where's Skeeter?" said Logan, looking for his dog.

Woof! Woof! Woof! They heard Skeeter's bark coming from the forest next to the creek. Logan marched into the woods to look for him. Tess and Anthony followed.

Just then Skeeter burst out of a thicket of witch hazel shrubs.

"Where have you been?" Logan asked.

Skeeter barked, spun around, and ran back into the shrubs.

"Skeeter! Wait!" Logan ordered.

The children ran after Skeeter.

"What is it, boy?" asked Logan.

Skeeter pointed his nose to the sky. Logan followed his gaze.

A flash of white rippled through the highest branches of the tree.

"D-did you see that?" Logan stammered.

"I think it was a ghost!"

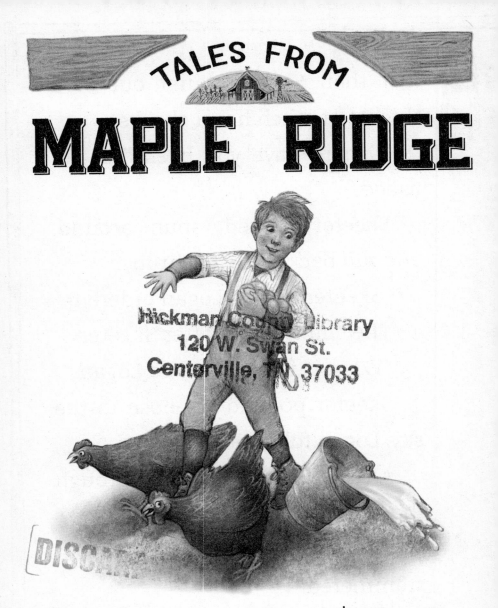

Find excerpts, activities, and more at
TalesfromMapleRidge.com!